The Restless

A Collection of Short Poems

Deepangsu Chatterjee

Ukiyoto Publishing

All global publishing rights are held by

Ukiyoto Publishing

Published in 2023

Content Copyright © Deepangsu Chatterjee
ISBN 9789362697509

*All rights reserved.
No part of this publication may be reproduced, transmitted, or stored in a retrieval system, in any form by any means, electronic, mechanical, photocopying, recording or otherwise, without the prior permission of the publisher.*

The moral rights of the author have been asserted.

This is a work of fiction. Names, characters, businesses, places, events, locales, and incidents are either the products of the author's imagination or used in a fictitious manner. Any resemblance to actual persons, living or dead, or actual events is purely coincidental.

This book is sold subject to the condition that it shall not by way of trade or otherwise, be lent, resold, hired out or otherwise circulated, without the publisher's prior consent, in any form of binding or cover other than that in which it is published.

www.ukiyoto.com

Dedication

For my parents Anup and Sumita - the sun and the rain, for Debasish - the wind, for Randall - the clear sky and Kritika for putting all of them together into this rainbow of mine..

Acknowledgemnt

My gratitude to Isvi Mishra and other editors and my publisher for their help and support.

I am thankful to Anindita Bose and Nikita Parik for their help in proof reading.

I am grateful to my family, friends and teachers for their faith and love.

Contents

Introduction	1
Section: Scream	3
The Boy Who Kept to Himself	4
The Smoking Gun	4
The Lamppost	5
The Fence	5
Six Bullets	6
The Needle	6
Independence Day	7
The Law	7
Power	8
The Speech	8
The Script	9
Education	9
Miracles	10
Score	10
Chains	11
Roots	11
Section: Woman	12
The Lady	13
The Mirror	13
Your Own Kids	14
Attention	15
Choice	15
Adventure	16
Commitment	16
The Key	17
Storm	17
The Accident	18

Section: Art 19

Painting	20
Ambition	20
Song	21
Flowers	21
Geometry	22
Show	22
Wisdom	23
Words	23
Act	24
Clicked	24
The Sculptors	25

Section: Surroundings 26

Rainbow	27
Morning	27
Leaves	28
Salt	28
Beach	29
Silence	29
Story	30
Wound	30
Paint Brush	31
Knowledge	31
Progress	32
Fireflies	32
Forest	33
Butterfly	33
Faith	34
Flow	34
The Sky	35
The River	35
Space	36

Section: Routine 37

Humor	38
Oblivion	38
Apology	39
Truth	39
Balance	40
Solitude	40
Money	41
Time	41
Shoes	42
Complaint	42
Salvation	43
Devoid	44
Shades	44
Moral Elevator	45
Winter	45
Project	46
Standards	46

Section: Conversation 47

Envelope	48
Right and Wrong	48
Blankets	49
Envy	49
Windows	50
Prison Walls	50
Parents	51
Disconnect	51
Whisper	51
The Wall Clock	52
Chess	53
Ladder	53
Negotiate	54
About the Author	55

Introduction

If you are not busy enough, you are not good enough; this is the world that we have built for ourselves with decadal consistent efforts. *The Restless* stabs a double-edged dagger of irony and calm through the heart of being perpetually busy. *The Restless* aims to identify the connection between human behavior across different scales of sentiments, reactions and conscience. The spatial and temporal variability of human beings fall apart, when it comes to the core of their nature that goes beyond any pretense, whatsoever.

The consistent change in the system we live in has been fruitful for some while perilous to others. Human-made changes have never been in a consistent timeline with changes observed in nature. Perhaps it is because we are too quick or maybe nature is too patient. *The Restless* offers a prism of perspectives to understand the evolution of such changes and their impact on our daily lives.

Introspection has been the most powerful tool for my well-being. It has been a process of decimating conflicts around me and finding possible reconciliations. The truth lies within and cannot be detached from us. One just needs to think. *The Restless* provides dense thoughts packed in a format of 4-5 lines to readers with a busy schedule. The thread woven around the words requires more thinking and less reading, the exact intent of this collection of poems.

The Restless comprises six different sections: Scream, Woman, Art, Surroundings, Routine and Conversations. Each of these sections has a theme laid out to the poems associated with them.

Section: Scream

The Boy Who Kept to Himself

People called him unsocial,

'Cause he never liked bantering.

One day, they found his body in the mud,

He wore a t-shirt that said, '*I will come back as a news anchor.*'

The Smoking Gun

He had a strange habit,

He liked staring into smoke coming out of a chimney.

One day, he could see no smoke;

The notice board at the factory entrance read, '*The owner was shot.*'

The Lamppost

The lamppost laughed at the road:
   "You're as gray and old as the next street."
The road replied with a smile:
   "At least people don't use me to put out their cigarettes."

The Fence

He saw his father and neighbor fight.
Over the fence around the backyard
since childhood, 'til the war,
When there was no house to fence,
And then they weren't fighting anymore.

Six Bullets

The man loaded his gun with six bullets.
Forty years back, when he joined the force,
He died on the street with a bullet in his head.
Later they found all six bullets in his gun lying beside him.

The Needle

He was scared of needles when he was ten,
He would cry out loud when the nurse would say,

"It is time" and bring out her gloves,

Last month he turned twenty, overdosed and died; the nurse said,

"He should have stayed scared of needles."

Independence Day

Once there was a single piece of land,
Nobody celebrated their Independence.
Then came greed, insecurity, torture and war;
Years later, people started marking their calendars.

The Law

They could never understand the Law.
It made so much sense to the ones who made them,
It also made sense to the ones who changed them;
They were told, both made sense in their own time.

Power

They tried egalitarian, democracy and communism,
They also tried dictatorship, and socialism,
They tried with religion and prayers too,
But could not stop the earthquake.

The Speech

They spoke English, French and Sanskrit to him,
They tried Arabic, Pashto and Urdu as well.
They wondered if Chinese, Japanese or Korean would work,
But he was not willing to listen.

The Script

The movie had no substantial message in it,
The audience said it was poor story telling.
The director said the audience wants entertainment,
Not a preaching sermon;
The producer and actors were happy though.

Education

The duty of the state and the strength of common man,
An avenue to add to the civil society,
If education is a social requirement,
Then why does money buy such a need?
And why not make us buy the air we breathe?

Miracles

What is not a miracle here?
The sun, the moon, the air we breathe,
The trees, the mountains, the rivers we drink,
The sky, the rain, the land we reap,
The violence, the bombs, the wars we wage.

Score

If the best things in the world are free,
How does one keep score?
And if it's a burden to keep score,
Why do we keep asking for more?

Chains

Seems to be made of steel, but it's all in the head,
Strength in sinew can only be as good.
As the strength in spirit and words unsaid.
Liberation happens when doubt is dead.

Roots

His grandmother had planted mango seeds in her yard,
She had died twenty years back.
The kids always had fresh mangoes growing up,
Until last week, when he got rid of the tree,
As the *roots* were cracking up the ground floor.

Section: Woman

The Lady

He wanted a girlfriend, and proposed to her,
She said yes.
For the rest of his life.

The Mirror

The mirror read 'Objects in the mirror are closer than they appear.'
She glanced behind and slowed down to get closer,
The crash got both of them off the road.
She shouldn't have slowed down.

Your Own Kids

She would stare at homeless little kids,
Playing on the grass at the park.
The doctors said she could never have one of her own,
Months later, she was busy dropping her kids at school.

Working Out

She bought a treadmill for her home,
On her way back from the store.
She heard a voice – most likely from the treadmill:
In six months, you could have walked to the Himalayas,
Instead, you decided to stay home.

Attention

She received a lot of attention for her looks
When she was young and bright,
Soon, her skin wrinkled and grew dull,
Her fans found someone younger.

Choice

The husband tried to live his ideals,
The wife tried to live hers,
They chose to grow together,
They chose *not* to grow apart.

Adventure

She was a rebel, couldn't hold on to roots,
Couldn't find peace in owning,
She left home without a penny
To embrace the bohemian life,
Only to learn that true joy was in sharing.

Commitment

He wanted to be committed to the truth.
His parents wanted him to be committed to the family,
His partner wanted him to be committed to her,
The taxpayers wanted him to be committed to his work.
He finally committed to the truth.

The Key

The box was *locked* and wasn't accessible,
She looked for the key, but it was nowhere to be found.
Probably he had the key when they separated, she thought,
Just their childhood photos were *locked* in the box.
She was glad she didn't have the key.

Storm

She's the joy of wind across all skies –
as She breezes over the lightning bolts,
Rustling leaves in a solemn dance,
Drenched in rain cleansing all dirt –
as She glides through skyscrapers, unbridled.

The Accident

Nostrils distorted, unaligned with the nose,
Cheekbones curved below her chin,
Twisted elbow and a bleeding forehead;
She still had a smile on her face.
Her child on the backseat was untouched.

Section: Art

Painting

They could not see through his art,
Mostly because they did not make sense.
Decades later they were sold in millions,
Probably because he was there no more.

Ambition

The teacher assigned her students to write on their ambition.
The six-year-old wrote, "I want to be:
A grasshopper when it shines, a fish when it rains.
A star when it's night and a bird when it's a day,
I want to be all; I want to be a poet!"

Song

A verse with beats and tunes sundry,
Sometimes betrayal, or realization of love,
Others, where Devotion hides and Truth seeks,
Sometimes serene as the autumn sky,
Adored, like the cradle of a sleeping child.

Flowers

They grow out of buds of a plant,
To end up sometimes in lovers' hands,
Sometimes as condolences over gravestones
And sometimes as delicious fruits.

Geometry

The structure of math our civilization rests on,
The face of design of all that's material,
The seed of shape, weight and size,
The elegant step to reality manifestation.

Show

The guitar solo that kept the crowd grooving,
The monologue that left the spectators in awe,
The dance that did not let anyone bat an eyelid –

They were just expressions, not meant for entertainment.

Wisdom

He had a wealthy father, a wealthy family.
Growing up, he had a ton of friends but no real ones,
He knew they talk behind his back, about his easy life.
They did not know about his wisdom,
Now he has a few, but *wise* friends.

Words

It started with stones in caves.
Until oak galls over parchment,

Then from feather quills on scrolls,
To the cursor on a screen.
Words never die.

Act

Which part of life isn't an act?
For a mother, when her child is born,
Or for a child when his parents are dead.
Is it the time when he falls helplessly in love?
Or when he plays his favorite character, in a show.

Clicked

I often wonder how to frame those moments
That went by cruising, unheeded and unclicked –

Do they have any importance at all?
Are these not to be savored like the ones we cherish?
In frames so grand with heaps of applause?

The Sculptors

The surgeons of art with *mud* in their hands,
And firmly shaped, with bones of clay,
With colors so bright that lit up her life,
And fine brush strokes for the eyes of grace.

Section: Surroundings

Rainbow

The symphony of colors with notes so high
When the sun meets rain,
What beauty lay so grand! When strangers
find their home in their other half.

Morning

Light creeps in through the curtain,
Brightening up her face in glow,
As she transcends from her world of dreams
To the mundane world around.
But, with a surge of joy and hope.

Leaves

They make food for all that's living,
They provide shelter to millions,
They make our air breathable,
Yet, they are just leaves.

Salt

It is not as special as cardamom seeds,
Not as distinct as cinnamon sticks.
Unlike pepper, has no dish named after it,
Isn't as bright and flashy as turmeric.
Even then, it is the crux of everything we eat.

Beach

Where the vast oceans get tired of running,
Where waves find their joy stumbling on rocks,
Where the Sun gets busy with its wide canvas,
We find not imperial stones, but castles of sand.

Silence

Silence is baffling yet it is vital,
It can be deafening, or peaceful at times,
Often used as a middle ground or to escape,
Often *unused*, by fools with little plan.

Story

Has your story of life been a tragedy?
Look around, you will find others –
been through worse.
If your story has always been fun,
Look around, you will find others have had better.

Wound

Like water through clay, it takes time
To seep through your skin,
Until you feel the same in your sinew.
It heals with time, early or late,
It does not follow the time you've set.

Paint Brush

Wiggly and furry is the squirrel's tail,
Curved up into a wave of curls,
She hurries down the tree into the meadow.
Like Nature's paint brush dipped in green
And strokes across the wisps of grass.

Knowledge

The quest of perceptions of scripted tales,
When gathered some, it feels like a lot,
And then when you gather some more,
Strangely, it feels like you know even less.
It is indeed the state of humble voyage.

Progress

The stairway to a greater good, but greater than what?
Two steps forward and one step back, is it all about footing.
And what about the other lanes, untried and barren,
Isn't existence itself the progress we all are seeking?

Fireflies

The nights with few stars, wait for light,
For flies like stars to light up the skies,
Floating through air like shooting stars,
And dancing though trees like wings on flame.

Forest

Carpets of green lie across lush fields,
Shrubs and plants, grass and trees,
And a family of a deer run across to find water,
As the rain soaks up the swamps there,
Rustling leaves old and new, in the night breeze.

Butterfly

Wings soaked in the mirth of shades,
As they set out to seek among flowers,
Here and there, the milestones of nectar
A dream for the caterpillar locked up in a cage.

Faith

It makes wonders when built around love,
And cripples those wonders when soaked in scorn.
It's meant to include and unite the living,
And not to establish a superior divine form.
It is best as a compass and not as the uniform.

Flow

Ever wondered how everything around us
Depends so much on its ability to flow –
Blood from the heart to the cells,
Water from the roots to the leaves
And the soul from life unto death.

The Sky

An endless ocean of air and clouds,
An open park for birds and flies,
To glide through the air and dive into rivers,
Weaving through storms, clouds and rain.

The River

Born in the mountains in sheets of ice,
To find its way into the sea,
Raising civilizations on its way,
With unbridled leaps through fragile borders,
Dancing through ridges with an eternal sway.

Space

How much space is space enough?

A farm, a yard, a town or a graveyard,

The heathen feathers lying cold on tombstones for days   —
Burnt them up to make more space.

Section: Routine

Humor

A biscuit of balance of words and weight –
Coated well, with a layer of wit,
Timed to the setting, to make it crisp.
Served to the audience with the right taste.

Oblivion

Actions fade into air, like buildings into dust,
Trees fall off the ground after years of patience.
Once a barbed wire, now has a lush green field,
And once a vast forest has turned into the Sahara –
While man thinks he will be remembered.

Apology

There is nothing wrong in trying and failing,
Or hurting one's friends on the way.
The path of reconciliation begins with admittance,
While apology goes longer than one can imagine.

Truth

The mystery of life we all do seek,
The sword of nature cutting through smoke,
The unmasked reasons of colorless light,
The lonely path of the fearless sight.

Balance

The pride of the acrobats in a circus,
The smile of the child riding a bike for the first time,
The calmness of the pilot gliding through clouds,
The patience of the single mom raising her kids.

Solitude

The greatest teacher of all times,
When you run away from the noisy crowd,
To envision paths you never knew existed,
To a space devoid of crosslines and darkness.

Money

A system of transfer evolved through ages,
Of skills, labor, intellect and art;
The metric of greed and ambition all around,
The shining carrot for our civilized cart.

Time

An abstract metric of actions and events,
Beyond the dimensions of space laid out,
The guardian of us all in the span of life,
Can expand or contract but doesn't go around.

Shoes

The grip of feet on roads unknown,
Flat and heels, soft and sharp.
Guardian of feet to keep warm and free
Of colors dull or bright, worn or dark.

Complaint

Twigs and leaves stitched together into nests,
Sand and mud packed in a colony of ants;
The brave cacti spend its life in the driest of soils,
And humans complain when the dishwasher breaks down.

Salvation

There is no single way to reach the peak,
Distinct are they in so many forms.
Yet no one way has enough strength
To make it through the whole sojourn.

Devoid

The blind man playing a soulful tune.
A myriad of colors on the canvas of the deaf,
Words of the wise scripted by the cripple;
At times, the grass on the other side is yellow and pale.

Shades

The palette of emotions resides in the mind,
Hide and seek of the dark and the light,
All that's life has been sewn with shades
Of love and abhor, of reticence and pride.

Moral Elevator

The climb to achieve the moral higher ground is futile.
As these morals reside over the wheels of time,
The higher ground doesn't look too pretty either,
They too have cracks, dust and sometimes too dry.
So, step out of this *moral elevator* for a life with less pride.

Winter

When leaves shed off their leaves and buds,
And the sky tucked in, with a gray blanket,
The squirrels stop running through the meadows,
And the rusty boat rests at the corner of the frozen lake.

Project

Excitement and passion takes the first row,
Experience and knowledge follow behind.
Mid-way through, they seem to reach stalemates,
Until a new idea climbs up the desk that seems right.

Standards

Nobody knows how they are set,
Yet *civil* society imbibe them in depth.
The ones who remain unperturbed
Are soon fenced in with the uncivil banner.

Section: Conversation

Envelope

It is the protector of the words we write.
In a piece of paper, we call the letter,
With stamps on its shoulders and glue on its lips,
A solemn promise of words sealed,
Destined to tear away into oblivion.

Right and Wrong

Who can tell what's right from wrong?
Do we learn that from the people around,
Or the roads we took, or the ones not taken?
What if right or wrong are just options?

Blankets

Strange are stains on blankets that lay –

Some unwanted, when they are marked with colors,

Some harmless as they blend into the blanket,

And turn the blanket to something we want to sleep on.

Envy

The kid thought he was devoid of envy,

And then he read about snow leopards climbing the Everest

With no jackets, air cylinders, lights or tents,

And camels striding across deserts, just like the next-door park.

He realized he wasn't all devoid of envy.

Windows

The opening to the other side of the wall,
A framed glimpse of the moving world;
She invites the moonlit night to seep in,
On sleepless nights with starry skies.

Prison Walls

Bricks of patience, have seen it all –
Murders, theft and gruesome acts,
Torture, suicides and silent kills,
With tales of trials, tears and deals.

Parents

The beacon of light in the "too" bright world,
The rudder for the ship of child's own sea —
As patient as the shores that bind the waves,
Aching as the tree uprooted in the storm,
When it's time for them to let go.

Disconnect

The loss of depth, with time that's gone,

Memories faded and moments unsung,

The witty have turned lame and dull;

What's left is just empathy for them.

Whisper

The warmth of breath held close to the ear,
An intense but short phrase of words
Goes straight to the heart and not through the head,
A smile of faith and eyes that obey.

The Wall Clock

The battery died and the wall clock ticked no more.
Dad and mom have their own wristwatch,
The children have phones to tell time.
The wall clock will find its way
From the storeroom to the auction table, someday.

Chess

The game of steps both swift and slow,
A battle of minds and not on field,
Wrapping the gray world with black and white –
A wonder world where the queen leads the king.

Ladder

The series of steps for the climb to the top,
And when the top is reached, there seems more steps,
Waiting to be climbed to a new top then,
Until you slip, pull yourself up, to climb again.

Negotiate

How much do we want and how do we take –
All that's there, isn't for sale,
And then there's the line of push and pull.
To convince them better or else just fail,
Often that's what makes someone pretty and someone lame.

About the Author

Deepangsu Chatterjee

Deepangsu Chatterjee is currently a Doctoral Student at the Washington University in St Louis. His work includes understanding processes that govern air quality from global to local scale using model simulations and satellite observations.

He was born in Kolkata and grew up studying mathematics and sciences. However, he could never let go of his love for literature. As a kid he published rhymes and short poems in local magazines. He published poems and essays in open access virtual platforms like 7tint, Terribly Tiny Tales and a few others.

The Restless is his first collection of poems. Currently, he lives in St. Louis, Missouri, USA.

www.ingramcontent.com/pod-product-compliance
Lightning Source LLC
LaVergne TN
LVHW041634070526
838199LV00052B/3355